WATCH OUT!

Tulika

सावधान!

TEXT Shamim Padamsee

PICTURES Ajanta Guhathakurta

TRANSLATION Veena Shivpuri

रचना शमीम पदमसी

चित्र अजंता गुहाठाकुरता

अनुवाद वीणा शिवपुरी

Watch Out! / Savdhan! (English-Hindi)

ISBN 978-93-5046-419-9
© *English text* Shamim Padamsee
© *dual language text* Tulika Publishers
© *pictures* Ajanta Guhathakurta
First published in India, 2013

Originally in English

Published by
Tulika Publishers, 24/1 Ganapathy Colony Third Street, Teynampet, Chennai 600 018, India
email tulikabooks@vsnl.com *website* www.tulikabooks.com

Printed and bound by
the ind-com press, 393 Velachery Main Road, Vijaynagar, Velachery, Chennai 600 042, India

"I'm going to get some food, children.
Take care of yourselves!"

"मैं खाना लाने जा रही हूँ, बच्चों।
अपना ध्यान रखना!"

"Let's play!"

"चलो, खेलें!"

"Let's pounce!"

"चलो, झपटें!"

"Let's drink!"

"चलो, पिएँ!"

"Let's climb!"

"चलो, चढ़ें!"

"Let's run!"

"चलो, दौड़ें!"

"Let's roll!"

"चलो, लुढ़कें!"

Grrrr!

"Let's eat!" says Ma.

"चलो खाएँ!" माँ कहती है।

"Let's sleep!"

"चलो, सोएँ!"